Woollies & Uggs

David Bateman Ltd
Unit 2/5 Workspace Drive, Hobsonville, Auckland 0618, New Zealand
www.batemanbooks.co.nz

ISBN: 978-1-77689-076-7

A catalogue record for this book is available from the National Library of New Zealand.

Book design by Lisa Allen
Printed in China by Toppan Leefung Printing Ltd

For Molly, who always knows her own mind — Emma Vere-Jones
For Madeleine Rose — Lisa Allen.

Woollies & Uggs

By Emma Vere-Jones

Illustrations by Lisa Allen

It was early December, a beautiful day.

On Raumati Street, kids were starting to play.

From number 14, there erupted a cheer.

'Put on your togs, summer is here!'

From the very next room, there came not a peep.

'Get up!' yelled Mum. 'We're off to the beach!'

Then out of their beds tumbled Billy and Roo

and Stella and Bella and Mallory, too.

They jostled and hustled and raced to the table.

They all took a seat as best they were able.

And last but not least, still snug in her rug,

came little Luella in PJs and uggs.

Five of the kids gobbled porridge and cream.

They sucked and they slurped, they blew at the steam.

But little Luella was up to her tricks,

she wanted to add something else to the mix . . .

'Luella!' cried Mum. 'No, no, no, NO!

'Marmite and porridge? It just doesn't go.'

'It does!' said Luella. 'I eat it MY way.

'Marmite WITH porridge for breakfast today.'

She took a big mouthful, then screwed up her nose.

‘That’s yucky’, she said. ‘It smells like Roo’s toes.’

‘Luella,’ sighed Mum. ‘Now do you see?

‘It’s really important to listen to ME.’

Once breakfast was over they bustled about,

washing and dressing, all keen to go out.

Then down to the car ran Billy and Roo

and Stella and Bella and Mallory, too.

In swimsuits and shorts and flowery shirts,

in dresses and sunhats, in jandals and shirts.

And right at the back, all wrapped up in rugs,

came little Luella in woollies and uggs.

Mum rolled her eyes. ‘Luella. No, NO!

‘You cannot wear that! Do you really not know?’

Luella stood firm. ‘I do it MY way!

‘Woollies and uggs are my clothes for today.’

With a look of defiance she hopped in the car.

'I'm ready,' she said. 'Is the beach very far?'

They rattled away with windows wound down.

Laughing and singing, they drove out of town.

But in the back seat, Luella was hot.

‘I’m sweaty,’ she cried. ‘I just want to stop!’

Mum gritted her teeth. ‘Now, do you see?

‘Next time, Luella, please listen to ME!’

They got to the coast and stopped with a screech.

Five kids and a dog raced onto the beach.

Then right at the back, in a bit of a fug,

came little Luella in woollies and uggs.

‘Put on your sunhats’, said Mum. ‘And your caps,’

‘Remember the sunscreen — the slip, slop and slap,’

‘Luella,’ she said. ‘Let somebody help.’

But it was too late. They heard the dog yelp.

Mum shook her head. ‘Luella. No, NO!

‘Put down the bottle and let the dog go.’

‘Luella,’ she said, ‘now, do you see?

‘I’ve told you before! You must listen to me.’

Down to the water dashed Billy and Roo

and Stella and Bella and Mallory, too.

They splished and they splashed, they danced in the sea.

Mum dived in too, laughing with glee.

But back on the beach, putting shells in a mug,

stayed little Luella in woollies and uggs.

Now, high in the sky something dark was occurring,

a wintery wind from the south was a-stirring.

Storm clouds had gathered and were heading their way.

It no longer felt like a summery day.

It started to spit, then that spit turned to rain.

Big heavy drops fell again and again.

Lightning and thunder crackled and rumbled.

Down from the sky huge hailstones tumbled.

Out of the waves scrambled Billy and Roo

and Stella and Bella and Mallory, too.

Their teeth chitter-chattered, their faces were pale.

They ran to the car to get out of the hail.

Mum ran behind, lugging everyone's gear.

Yelling: 'Crikey it's cold! We're outta here!'

Then as warm and as snug as a bug in a rug

came little Luella in woollies and uggs.

‘Mum!’ said Luella. ‘Now do you see?

‘Sometimes it’s good to listen to ME!’